More Poems and Stories from a Grandmother's Heart

More Poems and Stories from a Grandmother's Heart

KISHWAR MIRZA

ReadersMagnet, LLC

More Poems and Stories from a Grandmother's Heart
Copyright © 2022 by Kishwar Mirza

Published in the United States of America

ISBN Paperback: 978-1-959165-53-8
ISBN eBook: 978-1-959165-54-5

All rights reserved. No part of this publication may be reproduced, stored in a retrieval system or transmitted in any way by any means, electronic, mechanical, photocopy, recording or otherwise without the prior permission of the author except as provided by USA copyright law.

The opinions expressed by the author are not necessarily those of ReadersMagnet, LLC.

ReadersMagnet, LLC
10620 Treena Street, Suite 230 | San Diego, California, 92131 USA
1.619. 354. 2643 | www.readersmagnet.com

Book design copyright © 2022 by ReadersMagnet, LLC.
All rights reserved.

Cover design by Ericka Obando
Interior design by Dorothy Lee

TABLE OF CONTENTS

The Planet Earth	6
Race	8
The Alphabet	10
Elves	12
Monster in the closet	14
Ants	16
COVID 19	18
The Sun and the Moon	22
Ghost of Christmas	26
Wash your hands	30

The Planet Earth

The earth said to the sun
What is gonna happen when you're done
Who's working to keep the sky clear
and the dark clouds away
Who's gonna make sure it's a clear day
The sun shrugged and said I wish I knew
I hope the human race can come through
The ice is melting and the seas are no longer clean
The trees are dying and nothing is becoming green
The birds are screeching all around
No plants are coming up from the ground
The earth shook his head
He didn't want to be dead
He hoped people would sit up and pay attention
Get everyone out there and make sure to mention
What a lively planet he used to be
Let's go back and see
Birds flying from tree to tree
The morning air fresh and smoke free
A large wish to achieve
Can't be done without you and me.
So let's all take a stand
Hold each other's hand
Make sure the earth is left in a good way
Starting from today

 Race

The tortoise and hare had a race
The hare knew he would win, so he set the pace
They started at the line
The tortoise and the hare everything seemed fine
They get ready set to run
The starter fires the gun
The hare runs off; he is so fast
The tortoise starts he knows he is last
The tortoise moves one leg after another
It was hard getting them all together
The hare goes on his way
The sun is shining it's a beautiful day
The tortoise continues at his slo.o.ow pace
The hare runs back to him with a smile on his face
Come on old chap he says with a big grin
You know the way you move, you'll never win
The tortoise looks down and just continues to walk
He has no time to listen to the silly hare's talk
The hare runs off, it so hot
Knowing the tortoise will take time, he sits in a cool spot
He suddenly wakes up to a noise of loud cheering
What's going on, his head is twirling
He looks and sees the tortoise; he's almost there
Oh no that's not how it goes, it is not fair
The animals shout hurrah
and praise the tortoise's steady trot
He has won and the hare has not
The hare comes and wishes the tortoise well
It's a story he will live long to tell

The Alphabet

A is for Apple for all to see
B is a bat sleeping in the tree
C is for the caterpillar red yellow and green
D is for a dog with smile so white and clean
E is for elephant with a trunk so long
F is for a fox who loves to whistle and sing a song
G is for a giraffe who chews on leaves
H is for a hare with a hobbling tail blowing in the breeze
I is for ice floating in the sea
J is for jaguar looking at me.
K is for a kanga and roo sitting close by
L is for llama with woolly skin oh my!
M is for a mouse running across the floor
N is for a newt standing by the door
O is for orange a colour so bright
P is for pear a fruit so sweet and light
Q is for queen sitting on her throne
R is for ring on the cell phone
S is for a swing hanging from the tree
T is for turtle swimming free
U is for an umbrella standing open on the ground
V is for vacuum pushing all around
W is for a walrus big fat and sleek
X is for xylophone for me to keep
Y is for you listening to this rhyme
Z is for zebra dancing like a mime

Elves

Three elves sat on a shelf
Hoping they would sell
Waiting for a boy or girl to come
Sitting alone was really no fun
They went and moved their hats about
They wanted to jump up and shout
Come and see us in the store
We are fun and can do so much more
A man walking by saw the elves
He wanted to play with them himself
Young at heart and filled with glee
He would sneak into the store to see
Gently lifting up the elves one by one
The fun had just begun
He moved their arms, he moved their legs
He even tried to move their heads
The elves opened their mouths as if to speak
Nothing came out not even a peep
The man looked as happy as he could be
His smile was the biggest I ever did see
He laughed and jumped around
His feet danced on the ground
The elves felt good to bring him joy
He was after still a boy
One of the elves them whispered in his ear
His eyes filled with tears
He then went and put the elf down

The other elves started to frown
What did you say that upset him so
We were happy playing with him you know.
I told him that we were happy that he came
I remembered playing all his elf games
The man left the way he came
He would never be the same

Monster in the closet

There is a monster closet I hear at night
Even when I cover my ears and close my eyes so tight
He comes creeping to my bed
I hear him rattling and shaking his head
I count one two three
I only want my mummy
I try and open one eye
Look around to see if he is close by
I hear a shuffling on the floor
The monster is opening the closet door
Oh please don't come here
My heart is pounding and I'm full of fear
Something jumps on top of me
I tried to get up and just be free
I hear a soft whimpering sound
It's my dog Jack he's come around
He will keep him safe and warm
Save me from the monster's harm
Oh Jack I love you so
I don't want you to ever go
Jack lays his head down
I can now sleep without a frown
I hear steps shuffle away
The monster in the closet will have wait for another day

Ants

The ants went marching up the hill
They went marching one by one
When I saw them coming I thought I had to run
The ants came marching two by two
I didn't know what to do
The ants came marching three by three
They started to come to me
The ants went marching four by four
I started looking for a door
The ants went marching five by five
It is great to be alive
The ants came marching six by six
I started looking for a stick
The ants came marching seven by seven
The sun opened up and the sky looked like heaven
The ants went marching eight by eight
They stopped and went over a gate
The ants went marching nine by nine
Some were swinging from a vine
The ants went marching ten by ten
They reached their home and went in

COVID 19

The COVID virus blew into town
It just went and wandered around
Looking for people here and there
Not really having much of a care

Seeing a group sitting at a table
It went and sat next to a man named Abel
Making his throat tight and his chest ache
When he stood up he started to shake

His friends began to worry
Abel looked very scary
His face was pale and his eyes teary
He was tired and weary

COVID smiled and floated away
Maybe he would stay around for another day
There were people all over the place
Standing close together with little space

He could get a man and a woman too
They didn't seem to care about what to do
He had read all the signs
But people love to whine

Why cover my cough
Who are you to tell me off?
Why should I use my sleeve?
It's you who's making me sneeze

Social distance is something I have to do
2 metres between me and you
And now I can't stay
You have really ruined my day

COVID heard this and smiled
He had everyone riled
Maybe he would stay longer
It just made him stronger

So if you want to ruin his stay
Listen to what health professionals say
Wash your hands and stay at home
Let's make sure that COVID won't roam

The Sun and the Moon

The Sun and moon went out to play
On a beautiful summer day
The Sun hid behind a cloud
While the Moon counted out aloud
The numbers jumped around and around
They floated to the ground
One two three four and five
They laughed and danced the jive
Six seven eight nine and ten
They were there and disappeared again
The Moon lifted up his head
Here I come he said

The Sun peeked and looked for the Moon
Should he come out so soon?
The Moon was moving close by
The Sun was going to move up in the sky
He wanted to get by the Moon
It was going to get dark pretty soon
Oh what should I do he thought
I don't want to get caught
He looked for a cloud close by
Try and get lower in the sky

Slip closer to the earth
Where at night he has his berth
The sun tried to sneak on by
He would at least give it a try

The moon saw the sun's disappearing ray
He wasn't going to let him get away
I see you he shouted to the sun
There is nowhere for you to run
They laughed and giggled as they ran to the line
A new day would start and they would be fine
The sun reached first and then came the moon
Good night said the sun it will be morning soon
He stretched and yawned and headed for bed
Good night said the moon as he rose up
and touched the sun's head.
The two friends walked waved and went out of sight
The darkness fell and the day turned into night

Ghost of Christmas

The ghost of Christmas past came to me
He was there for all to see
Christmas is a usually a time of cheer
Except with COVID it won't be until next year

The virus is so strong the whole world through
Poor Santa doesn't know what to do
The windows are locked and the doors as well
Santa even tried ringing a door bell

No one came out
When they saw him, they would shout!
Santa wear a mask and cover your beard
Reindeers wearing masks is so weird

Rudolph's red nose couldn't shine
With his light hidden he started to whine
The virus just laughed
It had everyone in a flap

Santa, the ghost and Rudolph were distraught
Santa didn't know what to do
with all presents he had brought
They stretched for miles and miles
He would never get to see the children's smiles

This virus has just ruined everything
Even praying together is considered a sin
You just can't go anywhere
The stores are closed and the streets are bare

The ghost of Christmas past said hold on and think awhile
We will just celebrate Christmas, in a different style
Being away from family is not so nice
Just make sure you wash your hands once or even twice

Think of the all the people you love and who love you
Wearing a mask helps them from catching the COVID flu
Keeping a safe distance can be hard
It's like trying to buy a Christmas card!

The ghost and Santa got into his sleigh
They would wait for another day
The sleigh flew up into the sky
A merry Christmas to all and to all a good bye.

Wash your hands

Wash your hands every single day
Try and keep the Corona virus at bay
Put soap on your right hand and cover with the left
Rubbing for 20 seconds is the best
The bubbles fly all around
Some gently falling to the ground
We laugh as it hits my nose
We know how this goes
Everyone is worried and scared of what's to come
Staying home is recommended for everyone
This virus is nothing to play around
Staying in one place is keeping me safe and sound
When out 2 metres apart is where we should be
Making sure Corona stays away from you and me.
I try my best and listen to those who know
I just want this virus to blow
Hope a strong wind knocks it out of sight
Until then let's hold on with all our might
So COVID you won't have us beat
A community strong and complete

10620 Treena Street, Suite 230
San Diego, California,
CA 92131 USA
www.readersmagnet.com
1.619.354.2643
Copyright 2022 All Rights Reserved

www.ingramcontent.com/pod-product-compliance
Lightning Source LLC
LaVergne TN
LVHW050139080526
838202LV00061B/6532